Special thanks to David Friedman, Dan Rea, Larry Cancro, Josh Taggert, Naren Aryal, Sarah McKenna, Chris Bergstrom, and Linda Pizzuti.

Wally the Green Monster's Journey Through Time
Fenway Park's Incredible First Century

Requests for permission to make copies of any part of the work should be submitted online at info@mascotbooks.com or mailed to Mascot Books, 560 Herndon Parkway #120, Herndon, VA 20170

PRT1111A

Printed in the United States.

ISBN-13: 978-1-936319-83-1
ISBN-10: 1-936319-83-7

www.mascotbooks.com

Wally the Green Monster's
JOURNEY THROUGH TIME
Fenway Park's Incredible First Century

™

Dustin Pedroia

Illustrated by Gabhor Utomo

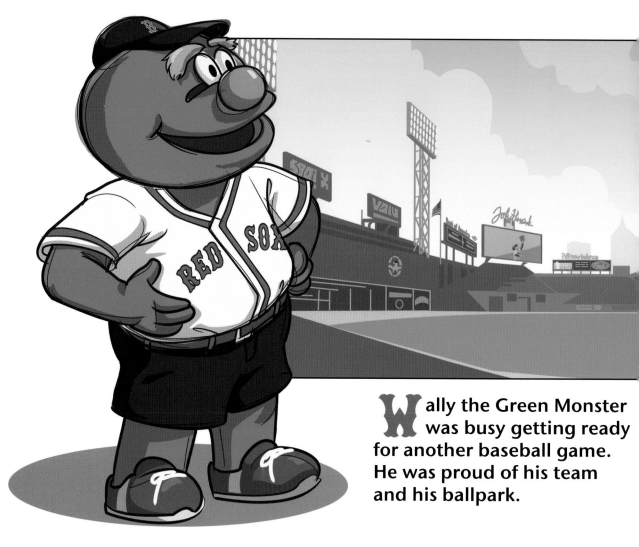

ally the Green Monster was busy getting ready for another baseball game. He was proud of his team and his ballpark.

FENWAY FUN FACT

Inside the Green Monster where Wally lives are small viewing slots that allow Wally to watch the game.

Just like the Red Sox players, Wally prepared for each game by running the bases, taking a few practice swings in the batting cage, and fielding a few ground balls. Wally practiced new cheers and thought of new ways to support his favorite team.

After his pre-game workout, Wally was exhausted! Fortunately, there was time to rest before the start of tonight's game.

As Wally was making his way back to his home in the Green Monster wall, something strange caught his attention. It was a bullpen cart decorated in Red Sox colors, but it was unlike any bullpen cart he had seen. The sleek cart looked like it was from the future, with antennas and mysterious gadgets. The mascot decided to take a closer look.

He sat behind the steering wheel, fastened his seatbelt, and turned the key. As Wally pressed the gas, the cart crept forward.

"Wow!" thought the mascot. Wally took the cart for a spin on the outfield grass, then onto the base paths. Around first base went the mascot ... by second ... rounding third ... then finally across home plate! Wally felt as though he had just scored a game-winning run in the bottom of the ninth inning!

FENWAY FUN FACT

Fenway Park seats up to 37,493 fans, one of the smallest parks in Major League Baseball.

As Wally crossed home plate, something amazing happened. Bright colors swirled all around, the bullpen cart shook and spun wildly, and it finally came to a halt.

Wally was confused.

He looked around and the first thing he noticed was that he was no longer in Fenway Park. Or was he?

Wally scratched his head — he could not believe what he was seeing: a façade of a ballpark under construction and a sign reading "Fenway Park." He noticed antique cars and horse-drawn carriages. This didn't look like the Boston he knew.

"Wait a minute!" thought Wally. "If that's Fenway Park being constructed, then it must be 1911!" The mysterious bullpen cart was actually a time machine that had transported Wally all the way back to when Fenway Park was being built!

FENWAY FUN FACT Opened in 1912, Fenway Park is the oldest major league stadium in the United States.

Wally couldn't believe that he had traveled back in time more than one hundred years! Before long, Wally was making friends and he even pitched in to help in the construction of Fenway Park.

1912

FENWAY FUN FACT

From 1912 until 1934, there was a 10-foot-high hill called "Duffy's Cliff" in front of the left field wall.

Soon, those swirling colors reappeared and Wally and his magical bullpen cart were transported one year into the future. It was April 20, 1912: Opening Day of the opening season of Fenway Park. Well-dressed men wore dark suits with black bowler hats, and women wore lovely dresses.

This old Fenway Park looked similar to the one Wally knew, but it was also different in many ways. The seats were wooden benches and some fans sat on the field near the outfield fence. And the Green Monster wall wasn't green! It was made of wood and was covered with colorful advertisements for local companies.

The umpire yelled "Play Ball!" and Fenway Park's first pitch was in the record books!

ally made his way back to the magical bullpen cart and stepped on the gas! He found himself right back at Fenway, but this time the year was 1919. The ballpark was packed and Wally noticed Irish flags everywhere. A distinguished-looking man was giving a speech. Wally discovered that the man was Eamon de Valera, who would become the president of Ireland.

1919

Moving forward to 1920, Wally next found himself ringside for the first of many boxing matches held at Fenway Park. Between rounds, Wally walked around the ring holding a sign that reminded the crowd what round was about to begin.

FENWAY FUN FACT The Red Sox won four World Series titles in their first seven seasons at Fenway Park.

Wally was having the time of his life! He had no idea that Fenway Park hosted so many important events. He hopped back into the magical bullpen cart, curious to learn more about the ballpark's history.

FENWAY FUN FACT

On January 5, 1934, a fire burned down much of Fenway Park, but it was rebuilt in time for Opening Day on April 17, 1934.

his time, it was Opening Day 1934. The left-field wall, Wally's future home, had just been rebuilt, and was now made of metal. The wall stood thirty-seven feet tall, with a brand-new manually-operated scoreboard, the first of its kind. The mascot walked inside the wall and found an empty room. He knew this would be his home.

Wally walked out of the Green Monster and wondered why a football game was being played. Wally found himself at a Boston Redskins game and learned that the Redskins played at Fenway Park in the mid-1930s, as well as the Patriots in the 1960s. When the home team scored, Wally signaled *touchdown!*

Back in the bullpen cart, Wally continued his magical journey. This time, he stopped in the year 1944. President Franklin Delano Roosevelt was delivering a famous speech just a few days before the presidential election. The president even turned to the mascot during his speech and said, "God bless America, Wally!"

Ted Williams hit the longest home run in Fenway Park history on June 9, 1946, a distance of 502 feet. The seat where it landed is now a special red color.

Just as Wally was thinking about going off to vote, he leapt ahead to 1954 and a historic basketball game at Fenway. That's right, a basketball game! The world-famous Harlem Globetrotters were putting on an amazing display and entertaining the crowd. A star Globetrotter player handed Wally a basketball and said, "Swish, Wally!"

1960s

Wally was headed to the 1960s. In 1967, Red Sox fans were worried that the team might lose a lot of games, but the club made it all the way to the World Series! Their best player was Carl Yastrzemski, who led the league in home runs, runs batted in and batting average to win the Triple Crown. Wally yelled out, "Hello, Yaz."

I n 1968, Wally was back for another sporting event at Fenway Park. This time, it was a professional soccer match between the Boston Beacons and the Santos club from Brazil starring Pele, one of the best players ever to play the sport. Wally cheered hard for the home team and watched as a player booted the ball into the net. "Goal, Wally!" said the Boston player.

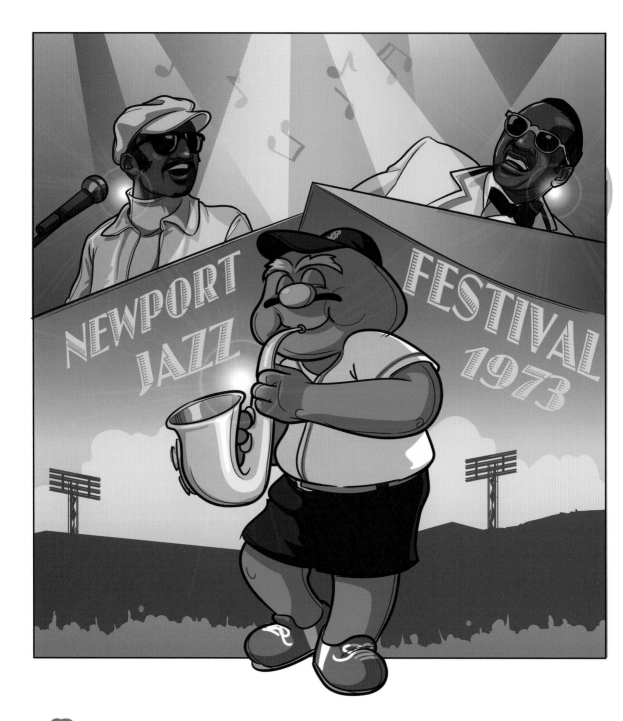

Before Wally knew it, he found himself at the 1973 Newport Jazz Festival, which took place at Fenway Park. Wally grooved to the sounds of Stevie Wonder and Ray Charles. Wally even picked up a saxophone and hit a few notes. Wally then requested that the talented musicians play two of his favorite songs: *Dirty Water* and *Sweet Caroline!*

ally grooved forward a couple years to the fall of 1975 when the Red Sox played one of the most exciting World Series ever. Carlton Fisk hit one of the most famous home runs in history, winning Game 6 with a 12th inning homer that bounced off the left-field foul pole. Although the Sox didn't win the championship, Wally felt prouder than ever about his hometown team.

1975

FENWAY FUN FACT   Fenway Park's right field bullpens where pitchers warm up were added in 1940.

2002

FENWAY PARK

1903 1904 1912 1915

SAVE FENWAY PARK !

FENWAY FUN FACT

In recent years, Fenway Park has truly "gone green" and seen many environmental improvements.

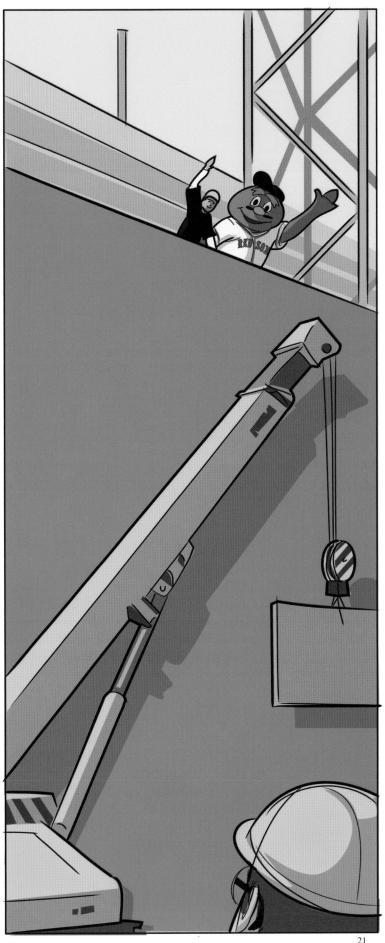

ally's next stop was 2001. As he strolled down Yawkey Way, he picked up a newspaper that said, "PLANS FOR NEW RED SOX HOME UNDER WAY." A wise old man explained, "Yes, they're thinking of replacing Fenway and building a new ballpark." Wally was worried – how could that possibly happen?

Then, in the wintertime, just around the holiday season, he learned that a new ownership group was buying the Red Sox. They hatched a plan to keep the team playing in Fenway, and to make the ballpark even better!

With Fenway Park's future safe, it was time to get back to baseball ... great baseball as the magical bullpen cart delivered Wally first to 2004 and then 2007 – and glorious World Series victories. Wally enjoyed reliving the amazing come-from-behind 2004 ALCS defeat of the rival Yankees, followed by the first Red Sox World Series victory in eighty-six years.

ust three seasons later, Wally was again on hand to watch the Red Sox claim their seventh World Series crown. The magical bullpen cart even took Wally to the World Series victory parades! Red Sox fans were thrilled to see their beloved team and their favorite mascot. Fans cheered, "We did it, Wally! World Champions!"

2007

WORLD CHAMP

RED SOX

FENWAY FUN FACT

Before the game, Red Sox players park their cars in their own private lot located on Van Ness Street.

FENWAY
FUN FACT
Fenway Park began its sellout streak of over 700 games on May 15, 2003, the longest sellout streak in baseball history.

As the World Series parade ended, the magical bullpen cart carried Wally back to present day Fenway Park. What an amazing journey it had been! Wally walked around the present-day Fenway Park – through the new open concourse behind the bleachers with all sorts of of yummy food stands, past the new large video boards in center field, then to the seats atop the Green Monster that sit above his home.

Now that he was back in Fenway Park, Wally wondered what he should do with the magical bullpen cart. Should he tell someone about it? Should he keep it a secret? He wasn't sure what to do, so he decided to move it into his home inside the Green Monster and make up his mind later. After all, it was almost game time and he did not want to miss a single pitch!

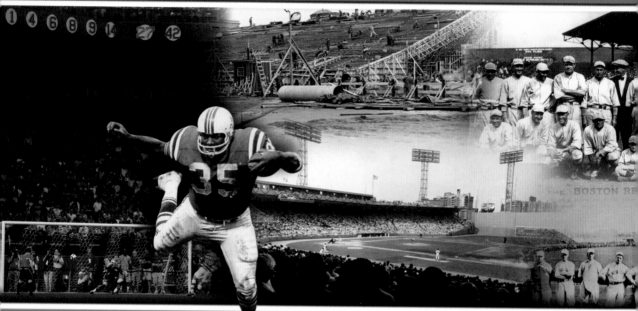

June 24, 1911 — Red Sox owner John I. Taylor announces that he will build a new home for the Boston Red Sox.

Late September 1911 — Construction on Fenway Park begins.

April 9, 1912 — Fenway hosts its first exhibition baseball game, with the Red Sox beating Harvard College, 2-0.

April 20, 1912 — Fenway hosts its first Major League game between the Red Sox and New York Highlanders. The Red Sox win 7-6 in extra innings.

October 16, 1912 — The Red Sox finish their first season at Fenway with a thrilling World Series victory over the New York Giants.

October 13, 1914 — The "Miracle Boston Braves" win the World Series at Fenway, which they had been using as a temporary home park.

September 11, 1918 — Led by star hitter/pitcher Babe Ruth, the Red Sox win their fourth World Series of the decade with a clinching victory over the Chicago Cubs.

1933/34 — Thomas Yawkey buys the Red Sox and rebuilds Fenway Park during the winter, creating the Green Monster in left-field.

September 22, 1935 — Fenway Park's largest crowd of more than 47,000 turns out for a doubleheader between the Red Sox and Yankees.

September 1941 — Ted Williams finishes one of the greatest seasons in baseball history by hitting .406.

1953 — The Red Sox and the Jimmy Fund create a partnership that has lasted to this day and continues with the annual WEEI/NESN Jimmy Fund Radio-Telethon at Fenway Park.

TIMELINE

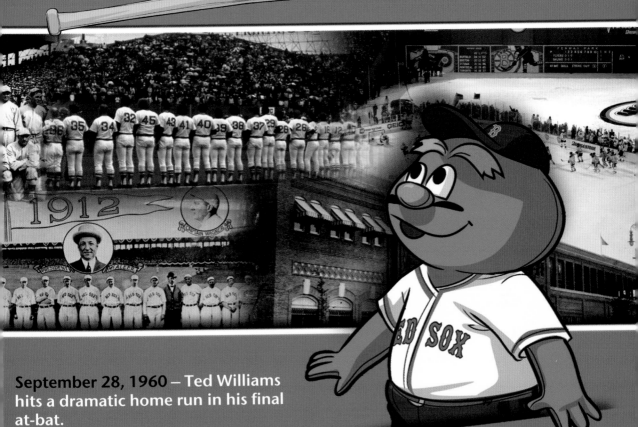

September 28, 1960 — Ted Williams hits a dramatic home run in his final at-bat.

1963-1968 — The AFL's Boston Patriots play six seasons at Fenway Park, one of several college and professional football teams that called Fenway home.

October 1, 1967 — The Impossible Dream Red Sox win the pennant on the final day of the regular season.

October 21, 1975 — Carlton Fisk hits perhaps the most famous home run in history, a 12th inning walk-off in Game Six of the World Series.

January 2002 — A new ownership group led by John Henry, Tom Werner, Larry Lucchino and Les Otten buys the Red Sox.

2002/2003 — 269 seats are added above the Green Monster, one of many Fenway improvements that take place from 2002 on.

September 2003 — Bruce Springsteen and the E Street Band play Fenway Park's first concerts in 30 years.

October 17, 2004 — Down three games to none in the ALCS, the Red Sox mount an historic comeback against the Yankees, then defeat the Cardinals in the World Series for their first title in 86 years.

March 23, 2005 — Red Sox ownership announces that the team will stay at Fenway Park for many years to come.

January 1 & 8, 2010 — Fenway hosts the 2010 Winter Classic between the Boston Bruins and Philadelphia Flyers on New Year's Day, followed by a college hockey doubleheader a week later. Fenway also hosts public and private skating.

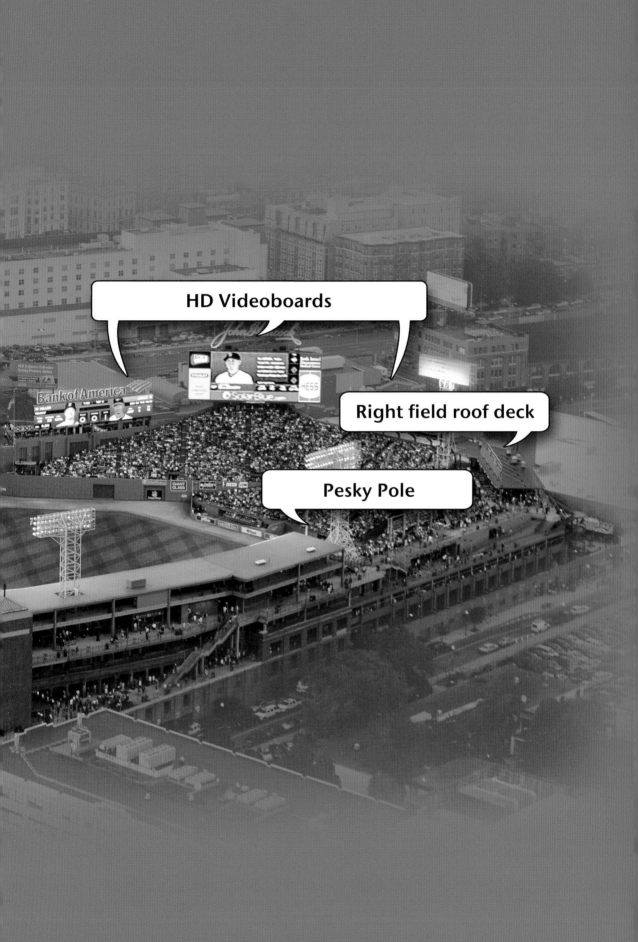

FENWAY
BY THE NUMBERS

37,493 Fenway's seating capacity at night.

37,065 Fenway's seating capacity during the day.

47,627 Size of the largest crowd in Fenway history (record set during a September 22, 1935 doubleheader against the Yankees).

7 Number of World Series the Red Sox have won.

12 Number of AL Pennants the Red Sox have won.

45 Number of Hall of Famers who have worn the Red Sox uniform.

3 Number of elephants at Fenway Park on June 6, 1914 purchased by Boston area children who raised money to buy elephants for the Franklin Park Zoo.

225,000 Bags of peanuts consumed per year (based on approximate 2010 totals).

1,100,000 Number of Fenway Franks consumed per year (based on approximate 2010 totals).

5,000 Number of new citizens sworn in at Fenway Park naturalization ceremony on September 14, 2010, the largest event of its kind in New England.

97 Professional football games played at Fenway Park (through 2011).

26 Professional soccer games played at Fenway Park (through 2011).

1 Professional hockey games played at Fenway Park (through 2011).

3,054,001 Total annual baseball attendance for 2011.